WHEN THE WORLD GOT SICK

Written by
Daniela Rumeo

Illustrated by
Michael Rumeo

Published by Daniela Rumeo
Toronto, Ontario, Canada
www.danielarumeobooks.com

When the World Got Sick
ISBN Number: 978-1-7772378-0-6

Printed and bound in Canada

For my late grandmother, Domenica Caro-Zambito,
and all other victims of COVID-19.

When the world got sick, a lot had to change.
I couldn't go to school. It felt very strange.

We had to stay home to lend a helping hand,
so the world could get better. We were taking a stand.

Mom and Dad said there were some things we couldn't do,
but we shouldn't worry, they had lots of ideas to get us through.

We couldn't perform our spring concert at school.
So instead, we had a singalong from our balcony, it was cool!

We couldn't go to Charlie's house to play.
So instead, we painted pictures for the hospital.
I made a stingray.

We couldn't go to the library to take out a book.

So instead, I read recipes with Mom and learned how to cook!

We couldn't go with Grandma and Grandpa to the mall.

So instead, we checked in on them with a video call.

We couldn't go to our favourite park.
So instead, we played in the yard with Max. He's got a loud bar

We couldn't go with our neighbours for a walk.
Instead, we wrote them messages on the sidewalk with chalk.

We couldn't go to the community centre for a swim.
So instead, we turned the basement into our very own gym!

We couldn't go with Dad to the grocery store.
So instead, we dropped off food at Ms. Caro's front door.

When the world got sick, I wasn't sad.
I knew we'd stick together, which made me glad.
We helped one another, you see that was the trick . . .
and the world got better, it's no longer sick!

THE END